The Boxcar Children® Mysteries

The Boxcar Children
Surprise Island
The Yellow House Mystery
Mystery Ranch
Mike's Mystery
Blue Bay Mystery
The Woodshed Mystery
The Lighthouse Mystery
Mountain Top Mystery
Schoolhouse Mystery
Caboose Mystery
Houseboat Mystery
Snowbound Mystery
Tree House Mystery
Bicycle Mystery
Mystery in the Sand
Mystery Behind the Wall
Bus Station Mystery
Benny Uncovers a Mystery
The Haunted Cabin Mystery
The Deserted Library Mystery
The Animal Shelter Mystery
The Old Motel Mystery
The Mystery of the Hidden Painting
The Amusement Park Mystery
The Mystery of the Mixed-Up Zoo
The Camp Out Mystery
The Mystery Girl
The Mystery Cruise
The Disappearing Friend Mystery
The Mystery of the Singing Ghost
The Mystery in the Snow
The Pizza Mystery
The Mystery Horse
The Mystery at the Dog Show
The Castle Mystery
The Mystery on Ice
The Mystery of the Lost Village
The Mystery of the Purple Pool
The Ghost Ship Mystery
The Mystery in Washington DC
The Canoe Trip Mystery
The Mystery of the Hidden Beach
The Mystery of the Missing Cat
The Mystery at Snowflake Inn
The Mystery on Stage
The Dinosaur Mystery
The Mystery of the Stolen Music
The Mystery at the Ballpark
The Chocolate Sundae Mystery
The Mystery of the Hot Air Balloon
The Mystery Bookstore
The Pilgrim Village Mystery
The Mystery of the Stolen Boxcar
Mystery in the Cave
The Mystery on the Train
The Mystery at the Fair
The Mystery of the Lost Mine
The Guide Dog Mystery
The Hurricane Mystery
The Pet Shop Mystery
The Mystery of the Secret Message
The Firehouse Mystery
The Mystery in San Francisco
The Niagara Falls Mystery
The Mystery at the Alamo
The Outer Space Mystery
The Soccer Mystery
The Mystery in the Old Attic
The Growling Bear Mystery
The Mystery of the Lake Monster

THE SOCCER MYSTERY

created by

GERTRUDE CHANDLER WARNER

Illustrated by Charles Tang

ALBERT WHITMAN & Company
Morton Grove, Illinois

Library of Congress Cataloging-in-Publication
Data is available from the Library of Congress.

ISBN 0-8075-7528-3 (hardcover)
ISBN 0-8075-7527-5 (paperback)

Published in 1997 by Albert Whitman & Company,
6340 Oakton Street, Morton Grove, Illinois 60053.
Published simultaneously in Canada by General Publishing, Limited, Toronto.

Printed in the United States of America.
10 9 8 7 6 5 4 3 2 1

Cover art by David Cunningham.

Contents

CHAPTER 1

Let's Play Soccer

"Oh, Benny, what are you doing to Watch?" Violet Alden asked her six-year-old brother.

Benny Alden grinned. He had tied a bandanna around Watch's head with a leaf tucked under one side to make an eye patch. "I'm a pirate," he said. "And I am making Watch walk the plank."

Benny had put a board across the stump that the Aldens used as a step up into the old boxcar in their backyard. He was standing on top of the board. Watch, who was a small black-and-white dog, was standing at one end of the board.

"Okay, Watch, jump off the plank into the ocean!" Benny commanded.

Watch looked over his shoulder at Benny. Then he sat down on the end of the board and yawned.

Ten-year-old Violet laughed. "I don't think Watch wants to walk the plank."

"I know," said Benny. "I'm not a very good pirate yet. I need more practice." Benny had been very interested in pirates ever since he and his sisters, Violet and twelve-year-old Jessie, and his fourteen-year-old brother, Henry, had visited Charleston, South Carolina. They had gone to help a friend of their grandfather's rebuild her house after a hurricane. But they had ended up finding a pirate's treasure.

Benny jumped off the stump. Without his weight on it, the board tipped forward.

"Look out!" said Violet.

"Woof!" said Watch, and jumped onto the grass as the board fell off the stump.

Benny and Violet both laughed now.

Watch ran in circles around Benny, wagging his tail and looking pleased with himself.

"Come on," said Violet. "You'll have to practice being a pirate later. Soo Lee is here."

Soo Lee was the Aldens' cousin. She was the daughter of Aunt Alice and Uncle Joe. They lived in Greenfield, too.

Violet, Benny, and Watch went across the backyard toward the kitchen door of the big old white house where they lived.

The red boxcar was the Aldens' old home. The white house was their new one.

After their parents died, the Aldens had run away. They had heard that their grandfather was a mean person. They'd made a home in the abandoned boxcar in the woods, where they had found Watch and adopted him.

Then Grandfather Alden had found them, and he hadn't been mean at all. So the four Aldens and Watch had come to live with their grandfather in his house in Greenfield. And he had even moved the boxcar to the backyard so that they could visit it whenever they wanted.

"Maybe Soo Lee would like to play pirate," said Benny.

"No," said Violet. "Soo Lee is here so we can practice soccer. She brought her soccer ball. We signed up for the Greenfield Summer Soccer League, remember?"

"I remember," said Benny.

"The tryouts are this weekend," said Violet. "We want to be ready."

She opened the back door and they walked into the kitchen. Mrs. McGregor, the housekeeper, was stirring something in a big bowl.

"Is that a cake for dinner?" asked Benny hopefully.

"It might be," said Mrs. McGregor with a twinkle in her eye. "You'll find out later."

"We're going to practice soccer with Soo Lee," said Violet. "At the park. May we get anything for you while we are out?"

"Maybe ice cream to go with the cake?" added Benny.

Mrs. McGregor shook her head. "Thank

you, but I don't need anything. Not even ice cream. Don't be late for dinner, now."

"We won't!" Benny promised.

Soo Lee, Henry, and Jessie were in the front yard. They were kicking a soccer ball back and forth. When Soo Lee saw Benny and Violet, she put her foot on top of the ball and stopped it.

"Come on," she said. "Let's hurry and practice." She gave the ball to Jessie, who put it into her pack.

When they reached the park, Jessie took the ball out of her pack. Then Soo Lee took another ball out of her pack.

"Two balls!" said Violet. "But you only use one ball to play soccer, don't you?" Like Benny, Violet had never played soccer before.

"Don't worry. We'll just use two balls for practice," said Henry. He, Jessie, and Soo Lee had all played soccer before. Soo Lee was a very good soccer player. She had played in Korea, where she was born. Like her cousins, Soo Lee was an orphan. Aunt Alice and Uncle Joe had adopted her.

Soo Lee, Jessie, and Henry showed Benny and Violet how to kick. Then they showed them how to run and kick the ball to someone else to make a pass.

"You can use every part of your body to move the ball," Soo Lee explained. "Except your arms and hands. Only goalies can use their arms and hands to catch the ball and keep it from going in the goal."

Soo Lee, Henry, and Jessie showed Benny and Violet how to kick the ball and keep it just in front of their feet on the ground as they ran forward. "When you move the ball forward like that," Soo Lee explained, "it is called dribbling."

Then Soo Lee and Jessie put their backpacks next to each other a few feet apart. "This will be our goal," said Soo Lee. "I'll be the goalie. You divide into two teams and play against each other and try to score."

Henry and Violet were one team. Jessie and Benny were another. They kicked and passed the ball and tried to keep it away from each other and shoot it into the goal. But no one could score. Soo Lee caught every shot they kicked toward the goal.

Then Henry stood at the goal. He caught every shot, too.

"You're good at the goal. And you're tall. You would make a good goalie," Soo Lee told him. "Maybe you should try out for that."

Watch sat on the sidelines and watched them play. Sometimes he barked. Then, suddenly, just as Benny got the ball and tried to kick it toward the goal, Watch ran out onto the field! He knocked the ball away from Benny. Then Watch began to push the ball with his nose.

Everyone stopped, and when they did, Watch pushed the ball right past Henry and into the goal.

"Yeah, Watch!" cried Soo Lee.

"Watch is a good soccer player, too," said Violet. She wiped her forehead with her sleeve. "Whew! I'm tired."

"We should stop. We don't want to be too tired to practice tomorrow," said Jessie.

Everyone agreed that it was time to stop. But before they could go home, they had to chase Watch to get the soccer ball back. He was very good at keeping it away from the others.

At last Benny caught him. "Game's over, Watch," he said, laughing.

As they walked out of the park, Violet said, "Soccer is not as hard as I thought it would be."

"You are doing really well, Violet," said Soo Lee. "So are you, Benny."

"Thank you," said Benny. He bent down to pat Watch on the head. "But you know who the best player is? Watch!"

"Woof!" said Watch.

CHAPTER 2

Which Team Is the Best?

"Gosh," whispered Violet to Jessie. "Look at all these people! What if I'm not on a team with anyone I know?" Violet was a little shy, and sometimes meeting new people made her nervous.

Jessie said, "I'm glad there are a lot of people. That means we'll have lots of teams. We'll make new friends, too."

"Maybe," said Violet. She still felt shy. But Jessie's words had made her feel better.

The day for tryouts for the summer soccer league had come at last. The sun was shining, and the grass of the soccer fields next to the community center was very green. Everywhere, children of all ages were racing back and forth passing soccer balls to each other. Others were dribbling up and down the field.

"Look," said Benny. He pointed to a girl who was bouncing a ball on the top of her foot. As they watched, she bounced the ball higher and caught it with the top of her knee. Then she bounced it even higher and made it land on her head. She bounced the ball on her head a few times, then let it drop to the ground, where she caught it with her foot again.

The girl smiled a little as she played with the ball. Her dark ponytail swung behind her, brushing against her golden yellow shirt.

"Wow," said Violet. "That looks like magic."

Henry nodded. "It's called juggling. She looks as if she has very good soccer skills."

Just then a tall man wearing a cap with a picture of a soccer ball on it called, "Attention! Could I have your attention, please?"

Some of the people trying out for the soccer league came over to face the man. But others kept on playing. The man pushed his cap back and smoothed his short blond hair. Then he stepped up onto the bottom seat of the bleachers, raised a whistle to his lips, and blew it loudly.

All of the players stopped running and talking then, and gathered around him at the foot of the bleachers. "Thank you," he said briskly. "I'm Stan Post. Everyone can call me Stan. I'm the director of the Greenfield Community Center Summer Soccer League. I'll also be one of the coaches. Now, I'll introduce our other coaches and go over a few things before we begin tryouts."

A boy with long blond hair and a red shirt said loudly, "This is so boring! I know all the rules."

"I don't know all the rules," said Benny, frowning at the boy.

"Shhh!" said someone behind them.

5

The boy rolled his eyes, but he didn't say anything else.

When Stan had finished introducing the coaches, he had everyone write their name on a name tag and stick it to his or her shirt. Then he divided everybody into groups. He had each group dribble and pass and shoot while he and the coaches watched. Stan wrote lots of notes on a notepad he was carrying. So did some of the other coaches.

Then Stan divided the groups into smaller groups and each of the smaller groups went with a coach to different parts of the soccer field.

"We're going to watch everybody for a little bit longer to make sure we put you on the right teams," Stan explained.

Violet was relieved to see that Jessie was in her group. She was glad that she knew someone. But she was not so glad that the boy in the red shirt was also in her group.

"Okay, everyone," said the young woman who was their coach. "I'm Gillian McPhee.

Everyone calls me Gillian. We're going to practice a few more drills — moves and skills that you use to play soccer."

Violet said softly, "What if you don't know how to do a drill?"

Near her, the boy in the red shirt gave a huge exaggerated sigh of impatience. Violet felt her cheeks grow red.

But Gillian only smiled at Violet. "If you don't know a drill, I'll explain it to you," she said. She looked at Violet's name tag. "Just do your best, Violet. That's what is important."

Violet smiled back at Gillian, feeling less nervous. Gillian had friendly brown eyes. Her dark brown hair was short and curly, and she was wearing tiny earrings in the shape of soccer balls. She was rather tall and her legs looked strong.

The boy in the red shirt said, "What's important is winning. That's what my brother Stan said. He should know, since he is in charge of the league."

Gillian glanced over at the boy. "Winning is important, Robert," she said. "But so is having fun and trying hard." She raised her whistle to her lips. "Okay, everybody, let's go. We're going to practice passing."

At the other end of the field, Benny, Soo Lee, and Henry waited as the girl in the yellow shirt sprinted up to them. Their coach, Craig Crenshaw, was having them run relays. He ran up and down the sidelines with each group of sprinters, talking all the time.

"Good, good, good," they heard him pant as he ran past. "Keep going, that's it. Good, good, good." His wiry legs flew as he talked, and his sunburned face grew even redder while his wild reddish brown hair seemed to stand out like the mane of a lion around his head.

Soo Lee ran forward with the next group. The girl in the yellow shirt stopped and bent forward to rest her hands on her knees, trying to catch her breath.

"Wow, you're fast," said Benny.

The girl straightened up and fanned her face. "Thanks," she said cheerfully. She reached into her pocket and pulled something out. "I think this helps. Red licorice. Would you like some?"

"Yes, thank you. My name is Benny," said Benny, pointing to his name tag. He stared at the girl's name tag, not quite sure he could read the word.

"My name is Elena," she said. "Elena Perez." She broke some licorice off for herself and chewed it.

"You're a good player, too, aren't you?" asked Jessie. "We saw you juggling a little while ago."

"I practice a lot," Elena said. "Someday, I want to play for the Olympic soccer team."

"You will," said Benny thickly, chewing on a big piece of licorice. There was admiration in his voice.

"I hope so," said Elena. "I have been practicing for it for six years, ever since I was six years old."

"Six years old! That's how old I am," said Benny. "Maybe I can be an Olympic soccer player, too!"

"Maybe you can, Benny," said Jessie.

"But now it's your turn to run."

Benny looked up and saw that Henry had just gotten back. He took off running as fast as his legs could carry him.

A couple hours later, Stan stood up on the bottom bench of the bleachers and called everyone over.

"Thank you," he said. "You have all tried hard and played well. The coaches will meet and decide which players are on which team. We will post the results on the community center bulletin board tomorrow morning when the center opens. The teams will have their first practice then."

Stan, Craig, Gillian, and the other coaches walked back toward the community center. They talked and gestured as they walked.

"Whew!" said Jessie. "That was hard work!"

"But it was fun, too," said Violet.

"I like soccer," said Benny. "But it makes me hungry."

"Me, too," said Soo Lee.

Henry said, "I'm really thirsty. Let's go

get a drink of water from the water fountain inside. The water will be good and cold."

"Good idea," said Soo Lee. "Then I have to hurry home for dinner."

The community center was almost empty because it was late in the day. Each of the five children took long, cool drinks of water. They were about to leave when suddenly they heard loud voices coming from behind a partially open door just down the hall.

"I don't care what you say, Stan. It is important for everybody to get a chance to play," said a man's voice.

Jessie, Benny, and Soo Lee exchanged looks of surprise. They had heard that voice a lot that day. It was the voice of Craig Crenshaw.

A woman's voice said, "Yes. Craig is right. Everyone who tried out today should be on a team."

"Gillian," whispered Violet.

"Putting beginners in the league is a waste of time," said Stan's voice. "In case you've forgotten, Anthony Della, the head coach at the university, is looking for an assistant coach. And having a bunch of beginners playing for you is not the way to get the job."

"It's unfair not to include everybody. This is a community league — " Craig said. But before he could finish, Stan interrupted him.

"I don't care if it's fair or not. I'm not letting a bunch of beginners stand in my way!" snapped Stan. The door of the office flew open and he stalked out. He marched down the hall toward the door at the other end. He never even saw the children standing by the water fountain.

A moment of silence followed. Then someone inside the office sighed. "He's right, you know, Gillian. Coach Della will be looking for assistants who coach winners, not beginners."

The door of the office opened. Gillian and Craig came out. "I know," Gillian said. Then she saw the Aldens and stopped in surprise. "Oh! Hello!"

"Hi. We were just getting some water," said Jessie quickly. She didn't want the two coaches to think that they had been deliberately eavesdropping!

Gillian hesitated, then said, "That's good. It's important when you are hot and have been exercising to drink lots and lots of water."

She and Craig walked by and went out the front door.

The Aldens followed slowly. Outside, Soo Lee said, "Good-bye. I'll come over early tomorrow and we can go to the community center together to see which teams we are on."

"*If* we are put on a team," said Violet. "I don't think Stan wants beginners like Benny and me to play soccer."

Jessie said, "We will all be put on a team. Don't worry."

"I hope you're right, Jessie," said Henry.

CHAPTER 3

"You'll Be Sorry!"

"You're not eating very much breakfast, Benny," said Grandfather Alden the next morning.

"I'm not hungry," answered Benny. "I'm worried."

"Worried? About the results of the soccer tryouts?" asked his grandfather.

"Yes. I'm not that good at soccer yet," said Benny. "I need lots and lots of practice before I can be as good as Elena Perez."

"Elena Perez? I know Dr. Perez and her husband, but I've never met their daughter Elena," said Grandfather.

"Elena is a very good soccer player," said Jessie.

"Yes," said Violet. "She'll definitely be put on a team. But what if players who are beginners — like me — aren't put on a team?"

She was thinking of the conversation they had overheard among Gillian, Stan, and Craig. If Stan had his way, beginning players like Violet and Benny wouldn't be allowed to play at all.

"If you aren't put on a team, none of us will play in the league, either," said Henry.

Just then Mrs. McGregor came in with Soo Lee. When her cousins offered her breakfast, Soo Lee shook her head. "Hurry," she said. "It's almost time to go to the community center to see which soccer teams we are on."

The Aldens finished their breakfasts quickly. Benny drank all of his orange juice and finished his cereal, but he didn't ask for seconds as he usually did. Although he felt better knowing that his brother and sisters would help him, and would not play soccer without him, he was still a little worried.

When they got to the community center, they had to make their way through a large crowd of children who had gathered around the bulletin board by the front door.

Robert Post pushed past them as they reached the lists of teams. “Ha,” he said to the boy who was with him. “I’m on the Bears. That’s Stan’s team and it’s the best. I knew I’d be on it. We’re going to win every game.”

Violet’s heart beat faster as she followed Henry, Jessie, and Soo Lee to the front of the crowd. She reached down and caught Benny’s hand.

Benny reached out with his other hand and tugged on his older brother’s shirt. “Am I on a team?” he asked.

Henry looked down with a big grin on his face. “You sure are,” he said. “You and Violet are on the same team, the Panthers. Gillian is your coach.”

“Yeah!” said Benny. He let go of Violet’s hand and waved his arms in excitement.

"Oh, good," said Violet. She was very relieved, and very happy, too.

"I'm on your team also," said Elena to Violet. She came up behind the Aldens and pointed over Jessie's shoulder to her name on the list. "I was on Stan's team — the Bears — but I asked to be put on Gillian's team. I like Gillian."

The Aldens saw then that Elena's name had been on Stan's list, but had been crossed out.

Jessie said, "I'm on Craig's team, the Hawks. I like Craig. But I don't know anybody on my team."

"Henry and I are on the Bears, too," said Soo Lee. "With Robert." She didn't sound very happy about it. "And look, Henry, you're going to be one of the goalies. Robert is going to be the other."

"Okay, everybody," said Stan. "Time for practice. Let's go!" He raised his silver whistle and blew it loudly.

Although Violet and Benny were beginners, they weren't the only ones on Gillian's team who were just learning to play soccer.

Gillian divided the fifteen players on her team into three groups. She put experienced players in each group to help teach the beginners how to play.

"Good, Violet," said Gillian, when Violet kicked a pass right back to Elena.

Then she showed Benny how to run and kick the ball better. She was very patient and Violet and Benny soon understood why Elena had wanted to be on the team that Gillian was coaching. They were learning a lot and it was fun, too.

Jessie, who was standing at the front of two lines of players, kept glancing over at Violet and Benny and Elena. They were laughing together and seemed to be having such a good time!

"Okay, team," Craig said. "We're going to do a drill to practice getting to the ball first. You won't be able to get a goal if you let players on the other team get to the ball first."

He stood between the two lines of players and held the ball up. "When I throw the ball out in front of me, I want the player at the front of each line to run out and try to get to the ball first. The first player who gets to the ball, wins."

Craig threw the ball. But Jessie hadn't been listening. She'd been watching her brother and sister on Gillian's team.

"Jessie!" cried Craig, throwing up his hands. "What're you doing? You have to pay attention!"

"Sorry!" said Jessie, and ran out to try to get the ball. But the other player got there first.

"That's okay. We're going to practice this some more so you can try again," said Craig. "But you have to pay attention."

"I will," Jessie promised. She did better after that, but she still kept glancing over at the Panthers.

Henry and Soo Lee were paying attention to what they were doing on Stan's team, but they weren't having fun.

Stan talked all the time, just as Craig did. Unlike Craig, however, he didn't say very encouraging things.

"That's terrible!" Stan shouted at Soo

Lee when she kicked a ball at the goal and missed. "You'll never win if you make stupid mistakes like that! Next!"

Behind Soo Lee, Stan's younger brother Robert snickered. "That *was* bad," he said as he ran past Soo Lee. Then he kicked the ball he was dribbling right into the goal and right past Henry. He turned to Soo Lee with a smirk on his face. "That's the *right* way to do it," he told her.

Stan didn't seem to notice that his brother was being a bad sport. He just blew his whistle and said, "Next!"

Henry and Soo Lee tried hard and did their best. But no matter how good anyone on the Bears was or how hard a player worked, Stan never said anything nice. "Run faster!" he barked. "Kick the ball harder!"

"This is awful," Soo Lee whispered to Henry.

"I know," said Henry, glancing over toward the other teams. "No coach on any other team is yelling like Stan is."

Robert overheard Henry. "Those teams

are losers," he said. "Forget about them. We're going to be the winning team."

Henry and Soo Lee looked at each other. Each knew what the other was thinking. If they weren't having fun playing, winning didn't mean anything.

At the end of practice, Stan said, "That's it for now. You've got a lot of work to do. You Bears looked like a bunch of clumsy bear cubs out there today."

"Come on," Henry said to Soo Lee. "Let's go tell Stan we want to be put on another team." As the rest of their team walked off the field, Henry and Soo Lee walked up to Stan.

"We'd like to be put on another team, please," said Soo Lee.

Stan looked down at Soo Lee and frowned. "What are you talking about?"

"My cousin and I would like to be on another team."

"Why?" asked Stan, frowning harder. "The Bears are the best team, and you are good players. Why would you want to be on another team?"

"Because we aren't having any fun," said Henry boldly. "We want to play on a team that is fun to play on."

"Fun? *Fun?*" Stan said, as if he had never heard the word before. "You're not supposed to have fun. You're supposed to win!"

"We know. But we want to have fun, too," said Soo Lee.

Stan put his hands on his hips. "Fine," he snapped. He pointed toward Gillian's team. "Go play on her team if you are not interested in winning. But I'm warning you, you'll be sorry!"

CHAPTER 4

A Soccer Team Spy?

Soo Lee looked over her shoulder as they walked across the field toward Gillian. Stan was still standing where they had left him, glaring after them. "Uh-oh," she said to Henry in a low voice. "Stan looks really angry."

"Then I'm even more glad that we're not playing on his team anymore," said Henry.

Gillian's team had gathered around her. "Okay, everybody, you all did a good job. If we keep working hard and really trying, we're going to have a terrific soccer sum-

mer," Gillian said. "See you at the next practice."

As the soccer players left, Henry and Soo Lee walked up to Gillian to tell her that they were now on her team. "Great," said Gillian, writing their names down on her clipboard.

"Hooray," said Benny, giving a little skip.

"I'm glad," Violet said.

"I'm going to be on your team, too," said Jessie.

The others all looked over at her in surprise.

Jessie went on, "I like Craig. I think he's a good coach. But I want to play with you guys on the Panthers."

With a nod and smile, Gillian wrote Jessie's name on her clipboard list. "Welcome to the team," she said. "See you all at the next practice." She tucked her clipboard under her arm and walked back to the community center.

"Does anybody need a ride home?" asked Elena. She pointed toward a car in the parking lot. "My father's here to pick me up."

"I'd like a ride," Benny declared. "My legs are *tired*!"

"We're going to get ice cream," said Elena.

"And my stomach is *hungry*," added Benny.

Jessie ruffled her younger brother's hair. "You're always hungry, Benny. Especially for ice cream."

"I'd like some ice cream, too," said Violet.

"I guess we do want a ride," said Henry. "Thank you."

The six soccer players began to walk toward Mr. Perez's car. As they got closer to the parking lot at one side of the community center soccer fields, Jessie said, "Look over there, at the other end of the parking lot."

They all looked. They saw a battered blue van with a man sitting in it behind the steering wheel.

"Isn't he holding a pair of binoculars?" Jessie asked.

The others turned and looked at the van.

Henry squinted a little and said, "I think you're right, Jessie. He *is* holding binoculars. And he seems to have them turned in this direction. But why?"

"Maybe he is watching for birds," suggested Soo Lee.

"A soccer field is a funny place to birdwatch," said Elena. "If I were a bird, I wouldn't stay on a soccer field. You might get hit by a soccer ball!"

Just then the man in the van put down the binoculars, backed quickly out of the parking lot, and drove away.

"Why did he leave so suddenly?" Soo Lee wondered aloud.

"Maybe he's a spy!" exclaimed Benny.

Henry laughed. "Oh, Benny," he said. "I don't think so."

Elena introduced them to her father, and they drove to the ice-cream parlor. The six children all got ice-cream cones and went outside to sit at the tables on the sidewalk to eat them. The ice cream tasted good after the long, hot soccer practice.

"Soccer makes me hungry," said Benny.

He had gotten chocolate ice cream with chocolate sprinkles.

"Me, too," said Elena, who was eating a butterscotch sundae.

"I'm glad I'm on a team," said Violet. "I didn't think Stan was going to let beginners play."

"What are you talking about?" asked Elena. She looked very surprised.

The Aldens and Soo Lee told her about the conversation they had overheard the day before.

"Well, Gillian should get that coaching job," said Elena. "She's a great coach. She's definitely the best one for the job."

"Ha," said a familiar, sarcastic voice.

They all looked up to see Robert standing on the sidewalk in front of them. "Gillian's a crummy coach," said Robert. "Stan is the best coach." He looked at Henry and Soo Lee. "Too bad you quit the Bears. Now you won't get a chance to win any games."

"We will, too," said Soo Lee. "Gillian thinks we are a good team."

"She's just saying that," said Robert. "I bet she's really upset. Coaching a bunch of beginners is going to ruin her chances of getting that job. The university is only interested in coaches who can coach winning teams."

He turned and walked away.

For a moment no one spoke. Then Jessie said, "Wow. He might be a good soccer player, but he is definitely not a good person."

"Robert would be an even better player if he were a better sport," said Elena.

But Violet wasn't thinking about that. She looked around at the others. "Do you think it's true?" she said. "Do you think that if our team loses, Gillian won't have a chance of getting that coaching job?"

"I don't know, Violet," said Henry. "I don't know."

It was two weeks later and the last practice for all three teams before the first game. Robert caught a ball and kicked it hard out of the goal and down the field where the Bears were practicing. "Gotcha!" he shouted at the player who had kicked the ball.

"At least we don't have to play our first game against the Bears," said Soo Lee.

"Yes. It will be much more fun to play against the Silver City Rockets," agreed Jessie. The next day all three teams — the Bears, the Panthers, and the Hawks — were going to play against teams at the Silver City Community Center.

Stan had started his team's practice early and was already yelling at his players. Gillian had gone to the room where each team kept soccer balls and equipment.

Now she and Craig were coming back to start practices for their teams. Each was carrying a big net bag full of soccer balls.

Craig walked over to his team and Gillian came to join the Panthers. "Okay, everybody," she said. "Each of you take a soccer ball and jog around the field. Practice kicking the ball as you run."

She opened the bag and turned it upside down, and the soccer balls came spilling out.

But they didn't bounce everywhere as they usually did. They thudded to the ground and just lay there.

"What is this?" asked Gillian, bending over to pick up a soccer ball. She squeezed it between her hands and frowned. "This soccer ball is completely flat," she said.

"So is this one," said Elena, picking up another ball.

"And this one," cried Jessie.

"They're all flat," said Gillian.

At that moment, Craig came running over holding a soccer ball in his hands. "Look at this! *Look* at this!" he cried. "Every single ball, flat. No air. Like a pancake. This is no coincidence. Someone let the air out of my team's soccer balls."

"Mine, too," said Gillian. She looked around at the Panther team members. "Is this someone's idea of a joke? Did someone sneak into the equipment room and let the air out of the soccer balls?"

Everyone on the Panthers shook their heads.

"Well, whoever did it, it's not funny."

Gillian's normally pleasant expression was cross. "We're going to have to pump all these balls up before we can begin practice."

"No one on my team knows anything about it, either," said Craig. He raised his hand and waved vigorously. "There's Stan. Stan! Come over here, please."

"What's the problem?" asked Stan as he approached the two coaches.

"This is the problem," said Gillian. She showed Stan the balls, and she and Craig told him what had happened.

Stan didn't change expression as he listened. When Gillian and Craig were finished, he said, "I wonder how that happened," as if he weren't really interested.

Jessie stepped forward. "Who has a key to the equipment room?" she asked.

Stan raised one eyebrow. "I do. Craig and Gillian do. So does the director of the community center, of course. And the janitor."

"Five people," said Henry.

"I hope you're not implying that one of us would pull such a childish trick," Stan said.

"Someone did," Benny said.

"Well, it could have been anybody," said Stan. "I unlocked the equipment door when I got here, a little before practice was scheduled to begin. I usually do that, and I don't lock it back up until after practice is over." Stan checked his watch. "If you'll excuse me, I have a team to coach."

"But what about our teams' soccer balls?" protested Craig.

"There's a hand pump in the equipment room," said Stan, sounding bored. "I suggest you get started."

"He wasn't much help," said Craig.

"No. But we'd better get started pumping up those soccer balls," said Gillian.

Craig, Gillian, and some of the players on each team took turns pumping the balls up as fast as they could. But it still took a long time. When it was finished at last, Craig's team took the balls back to their field and began to practice.

Gillian gave each Panther a ball. Still looking cross, she said, "Let's get this started. With our first game tomorrow, we need every minute of practice we can get." She glanced toward the Bears, who were practicing on the next field, and her expression was unhappy.

The Panthers had worked hard. They were better players than they had been. But the Bears were better still.

"Who would let all the air out of the balls?" asked Elena as they ran and dribbled their soccer balls. "That was a mean thing to do."

"Robert's mean," said Benny. "Maybe he did it."

"You can't just say someone did something because they're mean," said Henry. "You have to have proof."

"Maybe we can find a witness," said Jessie.

"We'll look for clues after practice," said Henry.

"I know who might have done it," said Soo Lee suddenly. "Look. It's the same blue van that was here before."

The van was in the same place, on the far side of the parking lot. They could see someone in it, but they could not tell if the person was using binoculars.

"Wow," said Benny. "Do you think the spy did it?"

"I don't know," said Henry. "But we're going to find out, as soon as practice is over!"

After practice, however, the van was gone. And when they asked Gillian if she had seen anyone suspicious-looking loitering near the equipment room, she shook her head. "I've thought and thought about it," she said. "But I don't remember seeing anyone near it before practice. Except, of course, Craig. He was on his way to get his teams' practice balls and I ran into him."

"It sounds as if almost anybody could have gotten into the equipment room," said Henry.

"Yes," Gillian said. "But I'm going to talk to Stan about keeping the door locked from now on. We don't need any more pranks like this." She fished around in the pocket of her windbreaker and brought out her car keys. "See you at the game," she said.

The Aldens waved good-bye to Gillian and to Elena. "See you tomorrow in Silver City," Elena called out the car window as she drove away with her father.

Then they went to get their bikes, which they had left along one side of the soccer field.

Violet picked up her bike and was about to get on it when she stopped. "Look," she said, pointing. "The blue van is over there now!" She wasn't pointing across the parking lot. She was pointing toward the road that ran down the other side of the fields.

"Yes!" said Henry. "I think that's the same van."

"The spy," said Benny, getting excited.

"Not a spy," said Jessie. "But I think we should ride our bikes in that direction to see if he has binoculars this time."

Quickly the Aldens got on their bicycles and rode around the community center and down the sidewalk along the road where the van was parked.

Just as they pulled up next to the van, the driver turned and looked out the window.

He had on dark glasses and a blue-and-gold cap pulled low on his forehead.

When he saw the Aldens, he started the van and drove quickly away.

The Aldens tried to follow him, but the van was too fast. By the time they got to the corner, it had disappeared from sight.

"He doesn't want us to see him," said Henry as they pulled their bikes to a stop. "That's for sure."

"But who is he?" asked Jessie.

"And why is he watching us?" added Violet.

"He had binoculars this time, too," Soo Lee said. "I saw them on the dashboard."

"Well, even if he isn't a spy," said Benny, "it's a mystery, isn't it?"

"It is, Benny," agreed Jessie. "But this time, it's a mystery without any clues!"

CHAPTER 5

A Missing Soccer Player

"The Silver City Rockets look like a good soccer team," said Violet.

"Good. They will be fun to play against," said Jessie cheerfully. "And look. There's even a locker room where we can change into our new shirts."

All the soccer teams had gotten new shirts in their team colors, with the name of the team and a number on each shirt. The Panthers' colors were purple and white.

Jessie, Violet, and Soo Lee went into the locker room. They each put their packs into a locker. They took off their sneakers and put on their soccer cleats and their new shirts. Then they hurried out to join the other Panthers on the soccer field.

The two teams lined up on opposite ends of the field. Then the referee blew her whistle and the game began!

"Go, Panthers!" shouted Grandfather.

Not everybody could play at once. Only eleven players from each team were allowed on the field at any one time. Benny didn't start out playing the game. He stood on the sidelines with Jessie.

They cheered loudly whenever the Panthers got the ball. Gillian clapped and cheered, too. Then suddenly Elena got the ball. She ran as fast as she could with it, dodged around one of the Rockets, and kicked it into the goal!

"Yeah, Elena!" shouted Benny. He looked up at Dr. and Mr. Perez, who were also standing on the sidelines. "She's a great player," he told them. "I'm going to be a soccer player like Elena someday."

Dr. Perez laughed. "I know you will, Benny," she said.

Just then, Gillian came over. "Benny, I'm taking Violet out of the game so she can rest. I want you to go in and play in her place."

Benny ran out onto the field. Someone kicked the ball toward him. He raced toward it and kicked the ball as hard as he could — and tripped. The ball skidded away. A Rocket team member fell over Benny and the referee blew her whistle.

"Tripping," she said, pointing at Benny. "The other team gets to kick the ball."

"I didn't *mean* to trip her," said Benny. But he got on his feet and backed up while the Rocket player kicked the ball.

Benny hurried up and down the field as fast as his legs would carry him. Soon he was very tired. He was glad when Gillian took him out and put someone else in his place.

At halftime, the score was tied, 1–1. "We have ten minutes to rest," Gillian told the

Panthers. "Everybody get a drink of water from our cooler."

Elena said, "Coach, I've broken one of my shoelaces. I have an extra one in my pack in the locker room."

"You can go get it," Gillian told her. "But hurry. We don't have much time."

Elena trotted toward the locker room.

Soon the referee blew her whistle. "Time for the second half," she called.

Gillian looked around. "Elena's not back," she said.

"Time," said the referee again as the eleven Rocket players went out onto the field.

"Jessie, you go in for Elena," Gillian said.

The second half began. Now Henry was playing at the goal. The Rockets kicked the ball toward him, trying to get it past him. But he caught every one.

On the sidelines, Gillian looked around with a worried frown. "Elena's still not back," she said.

"I'll go look for her," Violet volunteered.

"Thank you," said Gillian.

Violet ran toward the locker room. She pushed the door, but it wouldn't move.

Violet pushed again. The door wouldn't budge. "Elena!" Violet called. "Elena!"

"I'm in here," called a muffled voice from the other side of the door. "Someone locked the door behind me and I couldn't get out. I've been calling and calling."

Violet heard people cheering from the soccer field. She glanced over her shoulder. The Rockets had scored.

Oh, no, she thought. *I have to get Elena out to help the team.* "Don't worry!" Violet said loudly. "I'll get you out."

She looked up and saw that a bolt high up on the door had been locked. She tried to reach it, but couldn't.

Quickly Violet looked around. She saw an empty metal trash can nearby. She hurried over to it, picked it up, and carried it back to the locker room door. Turning the trash can over, she stepped up onto the bottom of it.

Now she could reach the bolt. She pushed the bolt back, jumped off the trash

can, and called, "It's unlocked!"

Elena burst out of the locker room so fast that she knocked the trash can over. "Thanks," she gasped to Violet, and ran toward the soccer field.

After setting the trash can upright again, Violet followed Elena. As she reached the sidelines, she heard Elena explaining to Gillian what had happened.

Gillian's eyebrows drew together, but she didn't say anything. She just sent Elena into the game to play in someone else's place.

The Panthers played hard. So did the Rockets. In the end, the Rockets won, 2–1.

When the game was over, Gillian told the Panthers to go shake hands with the Rockets. The two teams shook hands and then went off the field.

"I should have caught that last ball," Henry said. "Then we would have at least tied."

"You couldn't help it," said Benny. "You slipped, just like I did."

Gillian held up her hands. "Everybody

played very well today. I'm proud of you. But we have a problem. Somebody locked Elena in the locker room at halftime. Does anybody know anything about this?"

All the Panther players were silent. Then someone said, "Maybe the janitor or someone else locked her in by mistake."

Shaking her head, Gillian said, "No. The janitor would know to leave the locker room unlocked during a game.

"Well, if this is somebody's idea of a joke, it is not funny," Gillian said. Then she said, "See you at practice, Panthers."

Grandfather Alden came up to join them. "All of you are doing very well," he said.

"Thank you," said Benny.

"Go get your things out of the locker room," Grandfather said, "and we'll go home for lunch. I think Mrs. McGregor is cooking a special lunch to celebrate your first soccer game."

"We didn't win," Jessie pointed out.

"Did you play your best?" asked Grandfather.

They all nodded.

"Then it's worth celebrating," he told them.

The Aldens headed for the locker rooms. Players from all the teams were going in and out of the doors of the two locker rooms as they finished their games and got ready to leave.

Robert brushed by them as they reached the community center. "Out of my way," he snapped. "I'm in a hurry. We're about to start our game."

Then he stopped. "Too bad you lost your game," he said to Henry and Soo Lee. "I told you that the Panthers were a losing team."

"How did you know we lost our game?" asked Soo Lee.

"I got here early and watched. I watched the Hawks, too," said Robert. "They got lucky and won. But they're still losers, too."

Jessie could feel herself getting angry at Robert, so she said, "Aren't you in a hurry? I think I heard the referee blow the whistle to start the game."

Robert spun around and sprinted toward the soccer field.

"Oh, Jessie. Did you really hear the referee blow her whistle?" asked Violet.

Jessie grinned. "Yes," she said. "But I think it was a whistle to start another game, not the one the Bears are in. I just didn't want to talk to Robert anymore, though, did you?"

"No!" declared Benny.

"Someone locked Elena in the locker room at halftime and someone let all the air out of our soccer balls," said Soo Lee. "Do you think the Panthers are a bad luck team?"

"No," said Jessie firmly. "We're not a bad luck team. But I think someone wants us to *think* we are."

Just then Violet grabbed Henry's arm. "Look," she whispered.

Henry and everyone else turned to look toward the front of the building. "What is it, Violet?" asked Henry in a puzzled voice. "I don't see anything."

"It's him," she said. "It's the man in the blue van!"

CHAPTER 6

Follow That Van!

"The blue van? You saw the blue van?" Jessie cried.

"No! No, I saw the man who was driving the blue van," said Violet. She hesitated. "At least, I think it was him. He was wearing dark glasses and a navy blue cap with gold trim pulled down low over his face."

Henry said, "It could be him. But where did he go?"

"We should look for him," said Jessie. "But we have to hurry. Grandfather is waiting."

"We'll divide up. Violet and I will check inside the building, Benny and Soo Lee can check the parking lot, and Jessie, you go see if he's at the soccer field. We'll meet back here in five minutes."

The Aldens and Soo Lee scattered to look for the mysterious man. Five minutes later they had reunited in front of the locker room doors.

"Not in the parking lot," said Soo Lee.

"But his blue van is!" added Benny.

"We didn't see him anywhere inside the building," Henry said.

"Where's Jessie?" Violet asked.

"Here I am," said Jessie, hurrying over. "And I found him!"

"Where?" asked Henry.

"Most of the people watching the games are standing on the sidelines," Jessie said. "But a few are sitting in the bleachers. He's sitting up at the very top of the bleachers, in the middle of a group of parents."

"Do you think he is somone's father?" asked Benny. "Can someone's father be a spy?"

Jessie shook her head. "I don't know, Benny. He wasn't talking to any of the other parents. And he wasn't cheering for anyone. He was just watching."

"I think we should watch him," said Henry. "Let's ask Grandfather if we can stay just a little while longer."

Mr. Alden agreed that they could stay. "But we have to leave at halftime," he said. "We don't want to be late for lunch."

The Aldens and Soo Lee decided to split up again to spy on the man in the navy blue cap. "If we go over there all together," said Jessie, "it might make him suspicious."

Henry and Soo Lee went to stand behind the bleachers. Violet, Benny, and Jessie took seats at the top, at the end away from the man in the navy hat. They took turns glancing in his direction to see what he was doing.

But he didn't do anything. He just watched the Bears playing soccer against the Eagles, the Silver City team. And sometimes he didn't seem to even be watching.

Sometimes he stared down at a notebook in his hand and wrote in it.

"Is he studying for something?" asked Violet.

"Maybe he's writing spy notes in invisible ink," said Benny. "Then he's going to leave the book, and another spy will come along and pick it up and get the notes."

But when halftime came, the man put the notebook into the pocket of his windbreaker and stood up. He glanced around, and Jessie, Violet, and Benny froze. For a long moment, it seemed as if his gaze rested on them, but it was hard to tell because he was wearing sunglasses.

Then he walked down the bleachers.

Jessie jumped up to follow him. But just then, the man turned and looked back up the bleachers.

Quickly Jessie pretended she was just stretching. She sat down again. "I don't think we can follow him," she said. "I think he is suspicious."

"What are we going to do?" asked Benny.

"Don't worry," said Violet. "Henry and Soo Lee will follow him."

They waited until the man was out of sight, then jumped up and hurried down the bleachers. Sure enough, they could see Henry and Soo Lee walking a short distance behind the man as he headed for the community center.

"Jessie, Benny, Violet," Grandfather called across the field to them. "It's time to go."

The three walked across the field to join their grandfather. "Where are Henry and Soo Lee?" he asked.

"Here they come," said Violet.

Henry and Soo Lee came up to join the others as they went to the parking lot.

"What happened?" asked Jessie.

Henry made a face. "Nothing," he said. "The man just got into the van and drove away."

"I think he was suspicious of us," said Jessie. "Maybe that's why he left."

"At least we know it is the same man with the van," Violet said.

"Yes," agreed Henry. "And if he was here this morning, he could have been the one who locked Elena in the locker room."

"He was at practice when all the air was let out of the soccer balls," said Violet.

"I think he is our best suspect," said Soo Lee.

"Right now," said Jessie, "he is our only suspect. But we can't prove anything until we find out why he would try to sabotage the Panthers."

It was after lunch, and the Aldens had gone out to visit their old boxcar in the backyard. Mrs. McGregor had made a very special lunch for them. Benny had had seconds of everything. He'd eaten so much lunch that it had made him sleepy, and now he was lying in the grass next to the boxcar, his eyes half closed. Watch was lying next to Benny with his head on Benny's chest. He was waiting for Benny to wake up and play. Soo Lee had gone home after lunch. She had been yawning, too, when she left.

"Are you taking a nap, Benny?" asked Violet.

"No," Benny answered. "I'm just resting my eyes."

Henry, who was sitting next to Violet in the doorway of the boxcar, grinned down at his younger brother.

"What are you doing, Jessie?" asked Violet, looking over her shoulder at her sister.

Sitting at the table inside the boxcar, Jessie had her chin propped on both fists. She was staring at the wall with narrowed eyes. At first she didn't answer her sister.

"Jessie?" said Violet. "Jessie?"

Jessie blinked and looked startled. "I'm sorry. I didn't hear you. I was thinking too hard, I guess."

"What were you thinking about?" asked Henry.

"Everything that has happened to the Panthers," said Jessie. "I was trying to figure out who did it and why."

She got up and came to join her brother and sister in the doorway of the boxcar. Violet moved over to one side to make room for Jessie in the middle.

"Someone let the air out of the soccer balls on the last practice before our game," said Jessie. "Then someone locked Elena in the locker room at the Silver City Community Center at halftime."

"Maybe one of the players on the Rockets did that," suggested Henry. "Elena is one of the best players on the Panthers. Maybe they thought it would help make us lose the game."

Jessie shook her head and said, "I thought about that. But no one on the Rockets could have let the air out of the soccer balls before practice. They would have had to know when and where we practiced, who our coach was, *and* come early, all the way from Silver City."

"That lets the Rockets out," agreed Henry.

"The best suspect is the stranger in the blue van," said Violet. "He was at practice and he was at the game. So he could have gotten to the soccer balls and followed Elena and locked her up."

Henry said, "True. But you know what, I don't think he's our only suspect."

"You mean Robert?" asked Jessie.

"No. I mean Stan," said Henry. "He would have a reason to make the Panthers lose. He wants to make sure everyone thinks the Bears are the best team and that he is the best coach, so he can get the coaching job at the university."

Violet said, "Craig and Gillian want that job, too. Maybe Craig did it to make Gillian look bad."

"But someone let the air out of the soccer balls for Craig's team, too," Jessie reminded her.

"Maybe Craig did it so he wouldn't be suspected," Henry said.

"Or Gillian could have done the same thing," Jessie said. She held up her fingers and counted off the suspects. "Stan, Gillian, Craig, and the stranger," she said. "Four suspects. And not enough clues."

"Do you think anything else will happen at soccer practice?" Violet asked.

"I do, Violet," said Henry. "Either at a practice or at a game. We'll have to be ready. We'll watch Stan, Craig, and Gillian very closely. Then maybe we can catch whoever is doing this."

CHAPTER 7

Pop Goes the Soccer Ball

"Catch it, Watch!" shouted Benny. He kicked the ball toward Watch. Watch ran after it and pushed it with his nose.

Watch, Benny, and Soo Lee were practicing soccer in front of the Aldens' house. They were playing keep-away, trying to keep Watch from getting the ball. But Watch was too fast for them. Every time Soo Lee or Benny kicked the ball, Watch ran like a flash toward it and knocked it out of the way with his nose. Then Soo Lee and Benny had to chase him to get it back.

Soo Lee kicked a ball up in the air. Watch circled under it and when it landed, he pounced.

Then, suddenly, there was a popping sound, followed by a hiss.

"Oh, no!" cried Soo Lee. "Watch bit the ball!"

"He was just trying to catch it," said Benny. The two of them ran toward Watch, and Watch ran away, carrying the ball in his teeth. They chased him all the way around the house before they caught him.

"Good boy, Watch," Benny panted. He sat down on the front steps with the ball. He squeezed the ball between his hands. More air hissed out.

"Let me see," said Soo Lee. She took the ball and examined it. "There," she said. "See. There are two teeth marks in the ball. Those are Watch's teeth marks."

"I'm sorry," said Benny. "But it was an accident."

"I know. It's okay," Soo Lee said. She reached down and petted Watch. "He was just practicing. He'll know next time not to bite the ball, won't you, Watch?"

"Woof," said Watch.

"We came out to play soccer with you," said Jessie. She, Violet, and Henry came out of the house and down the front steps.

Soo Lee held up the ball. "We can't. My soccer ball has a hole bitten in it."

She and Benny told the others what had happened.

Henry inspected Soo Lee's soccer ball. Then he said, "We should go to the Greenfield Sports Store and get you a new soccer ball, Soo Lee."

"Yes," said Jessie. "If we put all our money together, we can buy you a ball to replace the one Watch popped."

"You don't have to do that," said Soo Lee.

"Yes, we do," said Violet. "Besides, how can we practice soccer without a ball?"

"Okay," said Soo Lee.

Benny took Watch inside to stay with Mrs. McGregor. Then they all got on their bicycles and pedaled into Greenfield.

The Sports Store was on a corner near the park. They parked their bikes outside and went in.

"Watch would like this store a lot," said Benny. "It has all kinds of balls: soccer balls, baseballs, basketballs, even tennis balls and golf balls."

"Do you think he would bite holes in all of them?" asked Soo Lee. She and Benny burst out laughing.

Jessie smiled. "It's a good thing we didn't bring Watch!" she said.

"There's a ball like yours, Soo Lee," said Henry. He and Soo Lee picked up the ball and examined it.

"It is just the same as the other ball," Soo Lee agreed.

"Then that's the one we should get," said Jessie. The five children headed for the cash register. They had just paid for the ball and were about to leave the store when Soo Lee said, "Isn't that our coach? Isn't that Gillian over there?"

"It's Gillian *and* Stan," said Violet.

Gillian was standing next to a display of

soccer cleats. Facing her, Stan had a matching sweatshirt and pants with the price tags dangling off of them.

As they watched, Stan shook his head and raised one eyebrow.

Gillian put her hand on her hip and scowled.

"I don't think they are shopping together," said Violet softly. "It looks as if they are having a fight."

Stan shook his head again. Gillian raised her voice and suddenly they could hear her. "That's not why I'm complaining and you know it, Stan. I like the Panthers. They are a good team. But you kept almost all the best players for yourself. You've made it nearly impossible for anyone else in the league to have a chance of winning."

"You're the one who wanted to let players of every skill level play together," said Stan, raising his own voice.

"I have a good chance at that job as assistant coach with Coach Della at the university, as good a chance as you," said

Gillian angrily. "Or I *had* a good chance, until you did this."

Stan smiled. It wasn't a nice smile. He said, "If you're such a good coach, Gillian, you'll be able to make the Panthers into winners, won't you?"

"You won't get away with this, Stan," Gillian said angrily. "I promise you, I'm going to find a way to stop you." She turned and stormed down the aisle.

Stan stood and watched her leave, both eyebrows raised, the unpleasant smile still on his face. "May the best coach win," he said finally, and laughed nastily before turning and leaving the store.

"I thought Gillian liked being our coach!" cried Benny.

"She does, Benny. But she's right. Stan did keep most of the best players for himself. There's not a single beginner on his team," said Henry.

"She really wants that coaching job at the university," observed Soo Lee. "It sounds as if she would do almost anything to get it."

"Anything?" asked Jessie quickly.

"Possibly," said Henry. "Maybe even sabotage her own team to cover up that she is sabotaging other teams."

"The only other team that has had bad luck is Craig's," said Violet. "And I don't think Gillian is behind any of the things that have happened."

"I don't, either. And anyway, Stan's team is the one she's mad about. Why hasn't anything happened to Stan's team?" said Benny.

"That's a good question, Benny. I don't know," answered Jessie. The Aldens went outside and got on their bikes and pedaled slowly home. After getting a cool drink of lemonade from Mrs. McGregor, they went into the front yard to practice soccer. They practiced all the rest of the afternoon. Whenever they rested, they talked about the mystery.

By the end of the afternoon, they were all better soccer players. But they were no closer to solving the soccer mystery.

CHAPTER 8

A Fake Phone Call

"Hello?" said Violet, answering the phone. She listened for a moment and a worried expression crossed her face. "The game has been moved?" she asked. "Oh. Okay. Thank you." She hung up the phone.

The Aldens were at the breakfast table. Benny wasn't eating as big a breakfast as usual because the coach had told the team not to eat too much before a game. The Panthers were playing the Hawks that morning. But he wasn't nervous, the way he had been before his very first soccer game.

Everybody else was calmer, too. Henry drank his juice and began to eat a second piece of toast. Jessie finished her cereal and said to Violet, "The game has been moved?"

"Yes. We were supposed to play at the Greenfield Community Center, but it has been moved to Silver City," she told the others.

Just then Soo Lee came into the kitchen. "Hi, everybody," she said.

"Would you like some breakfast?" asked Mr. Alden.

Soo Lee wasn't as nervous as she had been before the first game, either. "Yes, please," she said. "I'd like some juice. There's plenty of time for me to have some today."

"Not if we have to go to Silver City to play," said Jessie.

"Silver City?" said Soo Lee, surprised. "But we're playing at the Greenfield Community Center."

"Someone just called and told Violet that the game has been moved," Benny said.

Looking even more surprised, Soo Lee said, "No one called and told me that."

"Maybe they called after you left," said Violet.

"And maybe Aunt Alice said you were coming here and would find out from us," added Benny.

"I guess so," said Soo Lee.

But Jessie was becoming suspicious. "Did the person who called tell you his name?" she asked Violet.

"Nooo," said Violet slowly. "It was a man's voice. But it was very deep, almost as if he were trying to disguise it. I didn't recognize it, and he didn't say who he was."

Jessie got up from the table and went to the telephone. She looked up Stan Post's name in the phone book and dialed his number.

"May I please speak to Stan Post?" she asked when someone answered.

"This is Stan Post," he said at the other end of the line.

"This is Jessie Alden. Has the game between the Panthers and the Hawks been moved?" she asked. She listened for a moment and nodded. "I didn't think so," she said.

She hung up the phone and turned to face the others. "The game hasn't been moved," she told them. "That phone call was a fake. Someone didn't want us to go to the game this morning!"

"Who would do a terrible thing like that?" gasped Violet.

"The same person who let the air out of the soccer balls and locked Elena in the dressing room," said Henry.

"If it was a man who called, it couldn't have been Gillian," said Benny.

"That's true, Benny," said Violet. "I didn't think she would do any of those mean things, anyway."

"Then maybe it was Craig," said Soo Lee.

"Or Stan," said Henry. "Did he sound surprised when you asked, Jessie?"

"No. He didn't even sound interested," said Jessie. She made a face.

"Don't forget the mysterious stranger," Violet said. "He could have found out who we are from anyone and called us."

Henry put down his fork. "Whoever it was, maybe we should get to the game a little early today."

Later that day, the Aldens were at the community center. The Panthers were ahead of the Hawks 1–0, but Henry didn't want the Hawks to score even one goal. Henry was the goalie.

He paced up and down in front of the goal. He watched the teams running up and down the field.

Suddenly one of the Hawks kicked the ball toward the goal. Jessie ran after the ball. So did the Hawk. Who would get there first?

The Hawk player beat Jessie. He kicked the ball again.

From the side of the field, Henry heard Benny shout, "Go, Henry! Go, Henry!"

Henry ran toward the ball. The Hawk player ran toward the ball.

This time Henry got there first. He fell on the ball and curled himself around it so that the Hawk player could not kick it again.

He heard cheers from his team and from the sidelines as he got up. Looking down, he realized he was covered with dirt and grass stains from falling. But he didn't care. He had caught the ball!

The referee blew her whistle. The game was over!

With the ball under one arm, Henry trotted toward the middle of the field. All the Panthers shook hands with all the Hawks. "Good game," they said to each other. Gillian and Craig had taught both teams to do that. It was part of being a good sport.

Then Henry walked off the field with Elena, Violet, and Jessie, smiling broadly.

"Good catch, Henry," said Elena.

"I sure am glad you were there to save that goal," Jessie said.

"I think it must be scary to be a goalie," said Violet. "I don't think I could run and catch the ball like that."

Benny and Soo Lee ran out to them. They had played in the first part of the game but had not been playing near the end.

"That was great, Henry," said Benny. "I'm going to be a goalie!"

"I thought you wanted to be a forward like Elena and score lots of goals," Soo Lee teased her cousin.

"I'm going to do both," declared Benny.

"I'm sure you will," said Grandfather Alden as he approached.

"Keep up the good work, Henry," said Gillian. "The whole team played wonderfully. I am very proud of you." She applauded the team. Then the team applauded her. After that, everyone began to get ready to leave.

Craig came over. He shook hands with Gillian. "Good game, Coach," he said.

"Thank you, Coach," she said. "Why don't we go get some breakfast? I was too nervous to eat this morning before the game."

"Did you hear that?" whispered Benny. "Our *coach* was nervous!"

"Good idea," said Craig. They smiled at each other. Then Craig said, "I'll give you a ride. Then we can come back here and watch more soccer."

The two coaches walked to Craig's car, got in, and drove away just as Stan and Robert pulled into the parking lot. Craig and Gillian waved. Stan nodded. Robert stared straight ahead, ignoring them.

"He's being a bad sport, Grandfather," Benny said.

"He certainly is," said Grandfather.

"I'm learning a lot about soccer," Benny went on happily.

Grandfather Alden smiled and patted Benny's arm. "You all are," he said.

Just then Jessie, who had been staring across the parking lot, said, "I don't believe it! The blue van is here."

"Is the stranger in it?" asked Soo Lee. "Does he have binoculars?"

"I don't see anyone in the van," said

Jessie. She looked around. "I don't see the stranger anywhere."

The others looked all around, too. They didn't see him, either.

Grandfather Alden said, "The Perezes and I are going to go sit in the bleachers to watch the Bears play the Silver City Rockets."

"We'll come sit with you," said Henry. "But not right away."

Their grandfather's eyes twinkled. He knew that they were working on a mystery. But he only said, "Okay. See you soon."

As Mr. Alden and the Perezes walked away, Violet said, "If no one is around the blue van, maybe this would be a good time to go look inside. We might find some clues."

"Good idea, Violet," said Henry.

"Wait until Robert and Stan leave the parking lot," Soo Lee warned.

"Maybe we can look in Stan's car, too," said Jessie.

After the Post brothers had left the parking lot, the Aldens strolled over to the van.

They kept a sharp watch for the stranger, but they didn't see him anywhere.

At last they reached the van. Henry looked over his shoulder. "No one is in the parking lot," he said. "No one has even noticed we're here."

"Good," said Jessie. She led the way around to the other side of the van, so that no one could see them.

Looking inside, they could see that the van was neat and clean. A pair of binoculars was on the seat.

"Look," said Soo Lee. She pointed to a small sticker in the lower right-hand corner of the windshield.

"It's blue and gold," said Benny. "U . . . N . . . I . . . What does it say?"

"University," said Soo Lee. "It's a parking sticker for the university."

"Athletic Staff," read Henry, leaning over to examine the parking sticker, too. "See? Athletic Staff Number one-two-three-four-five-seven."

"Does the spy work for the university?" asked Benny.

"I don't think he's a spy, Benny," said Violet.

Suddenly Jessie said, "Someone's coming."

"Hide," said Henry. "Everybody duck down!"

They crouched low, so they couldn't be seen near the van. Nobody moved.

Was it the stranger? Had he seen them at his van and come back? Was he about to catch them?

CHAPTER 9

Trapped!

Footsteps crossed the parking lot. For a moment it seemed as if they were heading toward the van. Then, nearby, the children heard a car door open.

It stayed open for what seemed like a very long time. Then the car door shut and the footsteps moved away, back across the parking lot and out toward the soccer field.

Jessie let out a long, slow sigh of relief. She stood up so she could see through the van's window.

Robert was walking back toward the soccer field carrying his gear bag.

"Whew," said Henry. "It's a good thing we weren't looking in Stan's car. Robert must have forgotten his gear bag."

"Yes. And he would have caught us for sure," said Jessie.

"Maybe we should go," suggested Violet nervously. "There aren't any clues here."

The Aldens looked around the parking lot. But no one was there. In the distance, they could see Robert walking toward his team, still holding his gear bag.

The Aldens left the parking lot as fast as they could without running. They had just reached the far end of the soccer field where the Bears were going to play the Rockets, when Soo Lee said, "There he is."

They all stopped and stared. The stranger was walking toward them. As he passed Robert, Robert spoke to the stranger.

The stranger stopped. He didn't look pleased for a moment. Then he gave Robert a small smile and nodded.

"Look at that!" Violet gasped. "*Robert* is

smiling! And' it's a nice smile. I've never seen him do that!"

"I don't think anybody has," said Henry.

The stranger walked on. He came straight toward the Aldens. They kept walking, too.

He barely glanced at them as he walked by. But Robert stayed where he was a moment longer, staring after the stranger. Then he turned and went to join his team.

"Wow," breathed Jessie. "That really *was* a close call. If we had stayed much longer, the stranger would definitely have caught us."

"Does Robert know him?" asked Benny. "Is Robert working with the spy? Is Robert a spy, too?"

"It's a possibility, Benny," said Henry. "But I still don't know why. It doesn't make sense."

The Bears were standing on the sidelines. Robert straightened up as the Aldens and Soo Lee passed. Robert reached into his bag and pulled out his goalie gloves. He began putting them on.

Suddenly he stopped. “Oh, no!” he said.

In spite of himself, Henry stopped. “What’s wrong?”

“I don’t believe this!” said Robert in a loud voice. “Someone smeared peanut butter all over my goalie gloves. They’re ruined!”

“Peanut butter on your gloves?” said Benny. He wrinkled his nose. “Yuk.”

Stan came over. “What’s wrong here?”

Robert showed his brother the gloves.

“When did this happen?” Stan demanded.

“It must have happened when I left my gear bag in the car,” said Robert. “It’s the only time it’s been out of my sight. Someone was watching, and they went to the car and sabotaged my gloves.”

“Do you have another pair?” asked Stan.

“No,” said Robert. “I — ”

“Get a pair,” said Stan.

“But I — ”

“I don’t want to hear excuses. The game is about to begin. Just do it,” Stan snapped, and walked away.

"I have a pair of gloves you can borrow," said Henry.

Robert swung around to face them. He drew back his upper lip. "Oh, yeah?" he said, with a sneer in his voice. Then he looked past Henry. "You do?" he said, in a much nicer tone. "Would you mind if I used them? I'd really appreciate it."

"Sure," said Henry. He unzipped his own gear bag and took out his gloves. He handed them to Robert.

Robert smiled. It was another nice, normal, friendly smile. "Thanks, Henry," he said. "Thanks a lot."

He put the gloves on and ran out on the field to the goal.

"Why did Robert get so friendly all of a sudden?" wondered Soo Lee aloud.

"You did a good thing," Benny told Henry. "You were a good sport."

Henry laughed. "It's a lot more fun than being a bad sport. Come on, let's go sit with Grandfather." The Aldens headed up to the bleachers.

A gust of wind whipped across the field.

Bears

A familiar blue-and-gold cap suddenly whisked by Jessie's foot. She reached down and grabbed it. She turned and froze.

The stranger was standing right behind them. He was holding his binoculars in one hand. He held out his other hand to Jessie. "You caught my cap," he said. "Thank you."

"Y-you're welcome," said Jessie. She handed the man his cap, then turned and hurried after the others.

As they sat down, Jessie watched the stranger out of the corner of her eye. He climbed to the top corner of the bleachers and sat down. He pulled his cap down and raised his binoculars to his eyes.

She nudged Henry. "There he is," she said. "He was right behind us when you gave your gloves to Robert. I think he went to the van to get his binoculars."

"Hmmm," said Henry.

Violet said in a puzzled voice, "Who would sneak out to the parking lot and put peanut butter on Robert's gloves? It couldn't have been Benny's spy, could it have?"

"You're right, Violet, it couldn't have been," said Soo Lee. "We went into the parking lot just as Robert and Stan left it. And we were there the whole time, even when Robert came back to get his gear bag."

"Well, if the spy didn't do it, that means he didn't do any of those other bad things, right?" asked Benny.

Jessie's thoughts were whirling. "I don't know," she said. She put one hand on her forehead and tried to figure it out. She concentrated with all her might.

She lowered her hand and looked over at the stranger. Then she repeated, "I don't know who's done the bad things. But I think I do know how we can find out who your spy is, Benny!"

The man behind the counter was stuffing envelopes.

"Excuse me," said Jessie.

The man looked at Jessie over the tops of his glasses. "Yes?" he said.

"We'd like some information, please," said Jessie.

The Aldens had ridden their bikes over to the university. It had been a long ride, and they were very tired. Soo Lee hadn't been able to come with them.

"What sort of information?" asked the man.

"We'd like to find out who a car registration number belongs to," said Henry.

"Number one-two-three-four-five-seven," chimed in Benny proudly. "It's like counting, except that the last number is wrong."

The man got up from his desk and crossed the room to a file cabinet. He opened a drawer and rifled through some files. Finally he said, "Yes, we have a vehicle registered at the university under that number."

"Who is it?" asked Violet.

The man swung around and peered at Violet now. "Why do you want to know?" he asked. "Has there been an accident?"

"Not exactly," said Jessie. "I don't think the things that have been happening have been accidents."

The man peered at them all for a moment longer. Then he said, "I'm not supposed to give out that information without proper authorization."

"What?" said Benny.

"He can't tell us," said Henry.

"No," said the man. "I can't. Not without permission."

"How can we get permission?" asked Jessie.

"From the office manager," said the man. He added, "She's not in today. She'll be back tomorrow."

"Tomorrow!" cried Benny. "That's too long."

"That's the best I can do," said the man.

The Aldens walked slowly out of the office. They were very discouraged. They walked down the front steps of the building and across the campus to the bike rack where they had parked their bikes.

The university had big stone buildings,

smooth green lawns, and majestic oak trees lining the sidewalks. But the Aldens didn't notice.

"That's not fair," said Benny.

"We could ride our bikes back over tomorrow," said Violet.

"I guess that's what we'll have to do," said Jessie.

"No," said Henry. "We won't."

They all looked at him in amazement.

"Why not?" asked Violet.

"If the blue van is here," said Henry, "it is parked in the Athletic Center parking lot. Remember? It was an athletic staff parking sticker."

"You're right," said Jessie, getting excited. "And even if it is not there, maybe we can ask people who work there and they will know who the blue van belongs to."

"Yes!" cried Henry.

"Oh, good," said Violet as the Aldens got on their bikes and began to pedal to the Athletic Center. "I'm glad we don't have to ride our bikes all the way back here tomorrow."

As they reached the parking lot for the Athletic Center, Jessie slowed her bike to a halt. The others pulled up behind her.

Benny pointed. "There it is," he said. "There's the blue van."

"Yes, it is," said Henry. "And we're not going to have to ask anyone who it belongs to."

"Why not?" asked Benny.

"Because the parking place it is in has someone's name on it," Violet explained, staring.

"Who? Who is it?" cried Benny.

"Anthony Della," said Jessie. Then she read aloud the sign on the parking place where the blue van sat: "Reserved Parking. Coach Anthony Della."

Although it was a long ride home from the university, the Aldens didn't feel tired. They had too much to think about. When they finally did get home, they got a pitcher of lemonade from Mrs. McGregor and took it out to the boxcar. They sat on the grass next to the boxcar, with the pitcher on the stump, and talked about the mystery.

"Coach Della couldn't have done all those things," said Violet.

"No, he couldn't have," said Henry. "He has no reason to."

Benny picked up a stick and threw it for Watch. "Then why is Coach Della spying on us?" he asked.

"He's not spying on *us*, Benny," said Jessie. "But you're right, he is a spy."

Benny's eyes widened. "He is?" he asked.

With a laugh, Jessie said, "Not a bad spy, Benny. But remember? He is hiring a new assistant coach at the university."

"And Stan, Gillian, and Craig have all applied for the job," said Henry. "So Coach Della has been coming to watch them coach. But he didn't want them to know he was watching, so he has been careful not to be seen or recognized."

"But if Coach Della didn't do it, and Gillian didn't do it, who did? Craig?"

"Craig couldn't have been the one who put peanut butter on Robert's gloves," said

Henry. "Don't forget, Craig and Gillian had already left when Robert got there."

"And Robert said that the only time his gear bag was out of his sight was when he left it in the car," said Violet.

"But wait a minute," said Jessie. "No one came into the parking lot after Robert and Stan left Stan's car. We were there and we would have seen them. No one came near Stan's car except . . ."

"Robert!" said Henry.

"Robert? Robert is mean, but why would he do all those bad things?" asked Benny. "And why would he put peanut butter on his own gloves?"

"So no one would suspect him," said Violet.

Henry said, "But we've figured it out. And I think I know how we can trap him!"

"How?" asked Jessie eagerly.

"Like this," said Henry. "Listen . . ."

CHAPTER 10

A Soccer Trap

"Outstanding practice, everyone," said Gillian. "We're in good shape for the game with the Bears tomorrow afternoon. Go home and get some rest now."

Gillian slid her coach's clipboard into her gear bag, slung her bag over her shoulder, and walked to her car.

Henry picked up his own bag and walked over to Robert, who was standing on the sidelines of the next soccer field with his team. Soo Lee and the other Aldens followed.

"Did you get new gloves for the game?" asked Henry. Robert looked up and frowned.

"Yes," he said. "So if you were hoping I wouldn't, forget it. I'm going to catch every shot the Panthers try to kick into the goal."

"It's going to be an interesting game," said Henry. "I'm looking forward to it."

"Ha," said Robert.

Jessie said to Soo Lee in a loud voice, "You know what? I bet Gillian is looking forward to tomorrow morning even more than tomorrow afternoon."

"Why?" asked Soo Lee.

"Didn't you hear the good news?" Violet said. "Gillian has an interview for the coaching job at the university tomorrow morning."

"At eight o'clock," Benny burst out. "She's leaving at seven A.M. just to make sure she gets there on time."

"That's great," said Soo Lee.

Henry glanced over at Robert. "Good luck tomorrow," he said to Robert pleasantly.

"I'm not the one who's going to need it," said Robert. "The Panthers will. Especially your coach!" He turned and marched away.

"I think Robert believed us," said Violet softly.

"I think so, too," said Benny.

"We'll find out," said Jessie. "Tomorrow morning."

Watch yawned. "Shhh," said Benny. Then Benny yawned, too.

Henry looked at his watch. "It's almost seven A.M.," he whispered to Jessie.

"What if he doesn't come?" Jessie whispered back.

Violet said very, very softly, "I hear someone!"

The Aldens crouched lower behind the hedge along one side of Gillian's driveway. On the other side of the hedge, Gillian's car was parked in the driveway. They could see it by peering through the branches of the hedge.

As they watched, a figure on a bicycle

rode down the sidewalk toward them. The bicycle slowed down. Then it stopped.

Robert Post got off. He parked his bike on the sidewalk and walked slowly up the driveway. Once he stopped and looked all around, as if he suspected a trap.

No one moved a muscle. At last Robert started walking again. He reached the car and crouched down next to it.

"What is he doing?" whispered Violet.

Just then, they heard a hissing sound. Benny knew that sound. He had heard it when Watch had accidentally bitten a hole in the soccer ball. "He's letting the air out of her tires!" Benny cried, forgetting to keep his voice down.

Robert jumped to his feet. He looked wildly around. Then he sprinted toward his bicycle.

The Aldens ran after him. "Stop!" Henry cried.

Robert grabbed his bicycle. Watch ran past them all. He jumped at the bicycle and it fell over with a loud crash. Robert fell, too.

He looked up. The Aldens and Soo Lee had him surrounded.

"Your dog pushed me down," he said. "You're going to get in a lot of trouble for that."

"No, we're not," said Jessie. "You are the one who is in trouble."

"I — I don't know what you are talking about," said Robert.

"Yes, you do!" shouted Benny.

"You're the one who's been sabotaging the teams," said Violet.

"You let the air out of the balls. You locked Elena in the locker room," said Soo Lee.

"And you tried to make us think that our game had been changed," said Jessie.

"Why would I do that?" protested Robert. "Besides, someone tried to sabotage me! Someone put peanut butter on my goalie gloves."

"No. You did that. So no one would suspect you," said Henry. "You were the only one to go near your car when you'd left your gear bag in it. We know because we were in the parking lot and we saw you."

"Oh," said Robert. He sounded very much like a soccer ball that had the air let out of it.

"But why?" asked Violet. "Why did you do it?"

Robert pushed his bicycle to one side and got up slowly. He said, "I was trying to help my brother."

"How would doing all those things help your brother?" asked Soo Lee. "The Bears were winning anyway."

"I know. But I wanted to make sure he won. Stan's the best. I wanted it to look as if Craig and Gillian, especially Gillian, were careless and disorganized," said Robert. "I borrowed the key from Stan's key chain and slipped into the storage room one afternoon when no one was around to let the air out of the soccer balls."

"And you locked Elena in the locker room," said Benny.

"I hadn't planned on that," said Robert. "But I saw her going in as I was coming out of the boys' locker room, so I just locked the door behind her. It was so easy!"

"You called us, too, and disguised your voice and told us our game had been moved," said Violet.

"Yes," said Robert. "And when I heard that Gillian was going for an interview, I knew I had to stop her. But that wasn't true, was it? It was a trap, to catch me."

"You only did those things when Coach Della was around," said Henry. "Even that time when I lent you my goalie gloves and you were polite to me — it was only because Coach Della was standing right behind me."

"You know about Coach Della? Yes. I saw him and recognized him right away. But I didn't tell anyone. I decided this would be a good chance to make sure Stan got the job at the university. And I thought the only way for him to get the job was to make sure his team won every game. Winning is everything," said Robert. "That's what Stan says."

"It's not true," said Benny. "You were cheating and being a bad sport. And when you do that, you don't win."

Robert looked around at the five Aldens. "What are you going to do?"

"Call the police!" said Benny.

"No, Benny. We're not going to call the police. But, Robert, you have to tell Stan what you did. If you don't, we will. It was wrong," said Jessie.

"I know," said Robert. He picked up his bike. As the Aldens watched, he got on it and pedaled slowly away.

"We caught him," crowed Benny. "Didn't we, Watch?"

Watch barked happily. Then Benny yawned. "We caught him," he said. "And now I'm sleepy."

"Me, too," said Henry. "Let's go home and get some rest. We've got an important game this afternoon!"

"Go, go, go," shouted Grandfather Alden.

"Woof, woof, woof," barked Watch, wagging his tail and pulling at his leash.

Out on the soccer field, Benny, Violet,

Jessie, and Soo Lee played as hard as they could. At the goal, Henry tried to catch every ball.

"Good! Good! You guys are doing a great job!" Gillian shouted.

"Run harder! You can do better than that!" Stan shouted at his team.

Henry jumped for a ball. It hit the tips of his fingers and went into the goal.

The Panther fans groaned. But Gillian called, "That's okay! Keep trying."

Elena got the ball and ran down the field. She passed it to Jessie. Jessie passed it to Violet. Violet kicked it back to Elena. Elena kicked the ball into the goal.

Now the score was tied 1–1.

But the game was almost over. Everyone played harder than ever. Suddenly a Bear player ran down the field with the ball and kicked it into the goal, just past Henry's outstretched arms.

The score was 2–1. And that was how the game ended.

"We won, we won, we won!" chanted the Bears.

Panthers
Panthers
Panthers

Although they were disappointed that they had lost, the Panthers went out to the middle of the field to shake hands. Some of the Bears ignored them. But Robert led the others over to the Panthers. He shook hands with all the Aldens and Soo Lee. "Good game," he said.

As the Panthers walked off the field, Coach Della came up to Gillian. "Congratulations on a game well played," he said. This time, Coach Della wasn't wearing dark glasses and a hat pulled over his eyes.

"Coach Della!" said Gillian. "I didn't know you were here."

"I've been around," said Coach Della with a little smile. "And when you get a moment, I've got a job offer I'd like to discuss with you."

Gillian stood very still. Her cheeks got pink. "A job offer?" she said.

"Yes. I like your style. You aren't afraid to take challenges, and believe me, I know what a challenge it is to have a team with so many skill levels, from beginners to experienced players."

"Thank you," said Gillian, sounding stunned. "We didn't win very many games, though."

Coach Della smiled more broadly. "Winning isn't the only thing — although it *is* important. Come to my office tomorrow morning at nine and we'll work out the details."

"I'll be there," promised Gillian.

Coach Della nodded and walked back across the field.

"Hooray!" shouted Henry. "Hooray for Gillian!"

"Yes. You are a *real* winner," said Jessie.

"When I grow up," said Benny, "I'm going to go to the university and play soccer for you, Gillian."

"Me, too," said Elena.

"Me, too," said Violet.

Then the Panthers gave their coach a victory cheer. It had been a winning season after all.

"Hurry," urged Benny. "Or someone will get our seats."

He jumped out of the car and pointed toward the university stadium.

"It's okay, Benny," said Violet, catching Benny's hand. "The tickets Gillian gave us are special seats. No one else can sit in them."

"Are you sure?" asked Benny.

"Yes," said Grandfather Alden with a laugh. "We're sure."

"Hello," someone called.

The Aldens turned.

"It's Stan and Robert," said Soo Lee.

Sure enough, the brothers were walking across the stadium parking lot toward them.

"What are you doing here?" Jessie asked.

Stan said, "We came to watch the university's first soccer game of the new season. I'm glad we ran into you. Robert and I both have something to say to you." Stan put his hand on his younger brother's shoulder.

Clearing his throat, Robert said, "I'm sorry about what I did. It was wrong. And you were right, it was cheating and being a bad sport."

"And I was wrong, too," said Stan.

"Robert learned his win-at-all-costs attitude from me. I didn't realize how bad I had gotten until this happened. And until I lost that coaching job."

Henry held out his hand. He and Robert shook hands. Then all the Aldens shook hands with Robert and Stan.

"The game will be starting soon. We'd better get into the stadium," said Grandfather.

"Just one other thing," said Stan. "Craig got a job coaching at the university, too."

"Oh, I'm glad," said Jessie. "He's a good coach."

"And," Stan went on, "I've been asked to organize the Greenfield Community Center Summer Soccer League again next summer. It's going to be a league for everyone — all players. I want to make sure you'll join."

"Yes!" said Benny.

"Thank you," said Jessie. "We'll be there."

Then they all hurried into the stadium.

"There's Gillian!" said Violet as they sat down.

"Do you think she's nervous?" asked Soo Lee.

"I'm sure she is," said Henry. "But that's okay. She'll do a good job anyway."

"I'm still nervous before a soccer game," said Benny to his grandfather. "But it's not as bad. I'm getting better all the time. When I go to the university to play soccer for Gillian, I'll hardly be nervous at all."

The players went out onto the field. The referee blew the whistle and the game began.

Benny leaned over to his grandfather. "And don't worry," he told him. "If you don't understand anything about the game, just ask me!"

GERTRUDE CHANDLER WARNER discovered when she was teaching that many readers who like an exciting story could find no books that were both easy and fun to read. She decided to try to meet this need, and her first book, *The Boxcar Children*, quickly proved she had succeeded.

Miss Warner drew on her own experiences to write the mystery. As a child she spent hours watching trains go by on the tracks opposite her family home. She often dreamed about what it would be like to set up housekeeping in a caboose or freight car — the situation the Alden children find themselves in.

When Miss Warner received requests for more adventures involving Henry, Jessie, Violet, and Benny Alden, she began additional stories. In each, she chose a special setting and introduced unusual or eccentric characters who liked the unpredictable.

While the mystery element is central to each of Miss Warner's books, she never thought of them as strictly juvenile mysteries. She liked to stress the Aldens' independence and resourcefulness and their solid New England devotion to using up and making do. The Aldens go about most of their adventures with as little adult supervision as possible — something else that delights young readers.

Miss Warner lived in Putnam, Connecticut, until her death in 1979. During her lifetime, she received hundreds of letters from girls and boys telling her how much they liked her books.